Randy's Wings

By
Anne Troya

Illustrated by
Marla Chicconi

This is a work of fiction. Names, characters, places and incidents
either are the product of the author's imagination or are used
fictitiously, and any resemblance to any actual persons, living or
dead, events, or locales is entirely coincidental. This book was
printed in the United States of America.

To order additional copies of this book, contact:
Xlibris Corporation
1-888-795-4274
www.Xlibris.com
Orders@Xlibris.com

Dedicated to
Rudy, Nicole, and Natalie

Randy was excited. Uncle Jim was here
for a visit. Uncle Jim is a pilot who flies
cargo airplanes that transport zoo animals.

"Jim, have any of the animals ever
gotten loose on your airplane trips?" asked
Randy's mother.

"Not so far," he replied. "They were kept
in sturdy cages."

"Uncle Jim," Randy said, "I don't think
I could be a pilot."

"Why?" asked Randy's uncle. "I would
be afraid to fly the airplane by myself,"
he replied.

"Randy," Uncle Jim explained, "we are all
a little scared at times, but fear should not
hold you back from your dreams."

Randy's father chuckled as his brother,
Uncle Jim told of his adventures across the
sky. Randy's mother listened as well.

Uncle Jim's stories were so exciting, even
time seemed to fly. Although Randy was
wide awake, his mother thought it was time
for him to go to bed. "Tomorrow is going
to be very busy, Captain Randy, so march
upstairs and land yourself right into bed,"
his mother teased. Randy kissed his mother,
father and Uncle Jim goodnight and then
slowly walked upstairs.

As Randy went to bed, he thought about being a pilot just like Uncle Jim. He placed all his model airplanes on his bed, soaring the planes over and under the covers of his bed. The voices downstairs soon became faint whispers, and he could no longer fight sleep. As the night air blew upon his face, Randy's dreamy eyes rested upon the largest, shiniest airplane he had ever seen.

"Wow!" Randy gasped. He couldn't believe his eyes. Randy raced up to the top of the stairs and climbed on board. Inside the plane was a huge empty space without windows, or chairs for passengers. To his surprise, animal cages lined both sides of the airplane.

Uncle Jim tapped Randy's shoulder and said, "Randy, these animals are headed home to the zoo in San Diego. They performed in the San Francisco circus."

Randy petted the elephant's trunk, and asked his uncle, "Why is this elephant so sad?"

"That is Sally, the baby elephant. She misses her mother," Uncle Jim replied. "How would you like to be my co-pilot to San Diego?" asked Uncle Jim.

Randy's answer was a loud "YES" as he headed straight for the cockpit door.

The cockpit seemed larger than he
had imagined. The front panel had many
different levers and switches, even more
than he had seen on the airplanes at the
video arcade. The throttle looked familiar.
It looked like a broken steering wheel:
like on the boats at Playland.

Randy sat in the co-pilot's chair.
He giggled at the idea of being Uncle Jim's
co-pilot. As they readied for take-off,
his heart began to race as he realized that
this was the trip he had been dreaming of.

Just then a crackled voice came out of the radio speaker. "This is San Francisco ground control tower. Are you ready for take-off?"

"This is hard to believe," Randy whispered.

Uncle Jim spoke into the headphones. "Roger ground control. Can you give us taxi instructions?"

"Roger", responded the voice on the radio. "I have received clearance on runway 37."

Uncle Jim and Randy snapped their seat belts on. "All right co-pilot Randy," he said. "Prepare for take-off."

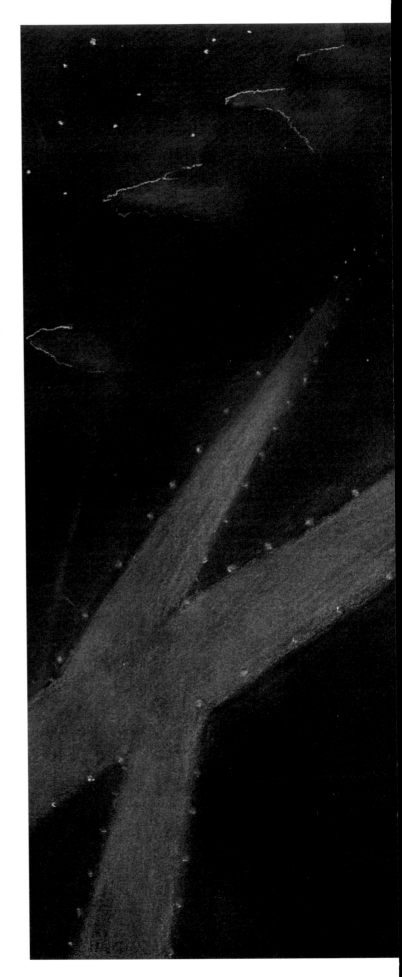

Randy never felt as excited as he was at this moment.

Uncle Jim was so proud to share this airplane trip with his nephew. Randy listened as Jim explained what each dial, lever, and switch did on the cockpit console. As they flew onward, Uncle Jim pointed out some of the landmarks far below.

Uncle Jim spoke into the microphone. "Air traffic tower, this is flight 301. We are on schedule." All of a sudden, a loud crashing sound came from the back of the airplane. Uncle Jim reached over and flipped a switch upward. "Randy," his uncle said, "this is the auto pilot switch. It flies the plane and keeps it on course. Stay here while I see what's happened in the back."

As Uncle Jim made his way to the back of the airplane, he discovered Manny, the chimpanzee was loose. Uncle Jim rushed to catch him but it was too late. Manny had managed to open the ostrich's cage. Uncle Jim had to gather the animals back into their cages. He started with the ostrich because he knew Manny was going to be a chore. Just as he placed the ostrich back in his cage, Manny let Sally, the baby elephant, out.

"Manny, stop that," Jim yelled. Manny ran and jumped on Jim's shoulders, covering his eyes with his huge chimp hands. Jim struggled and finally got Manny under control.

Just as he was opening Manny's cage to place him inside, Sally headed straight for the cockpit door.

Randy was startled as he watched the huge elephant thrust her body through the door.

"Oh no!" Randy yelled in surprise.

Sally came to a sudden halt: she could not fit through the opening.

Randy said to his uncle, "I think she's stuck. What should I do?"

Randy tried to push her back out, but it was no use. Sally would not budge. Sally lifted her trunk and let out a loud snort.

Uncle Jim tried to pull her back out into the cargo area. But soon he gave up. "I believe she is stuck for good," he said in frustration. "And I can't get through the doorway." There was no room for Uncle Jim to climb over or under Sally. "We will be in San Diego in fifteen minutes. You will have to land the plane by yourself."

"I can't. I can't," Randy said with a shaky voice.

"Listen, Randy," his uncle tried to remain calm. "I'll give you instructions from back here. And we'll also get help from the airport traffic tower."

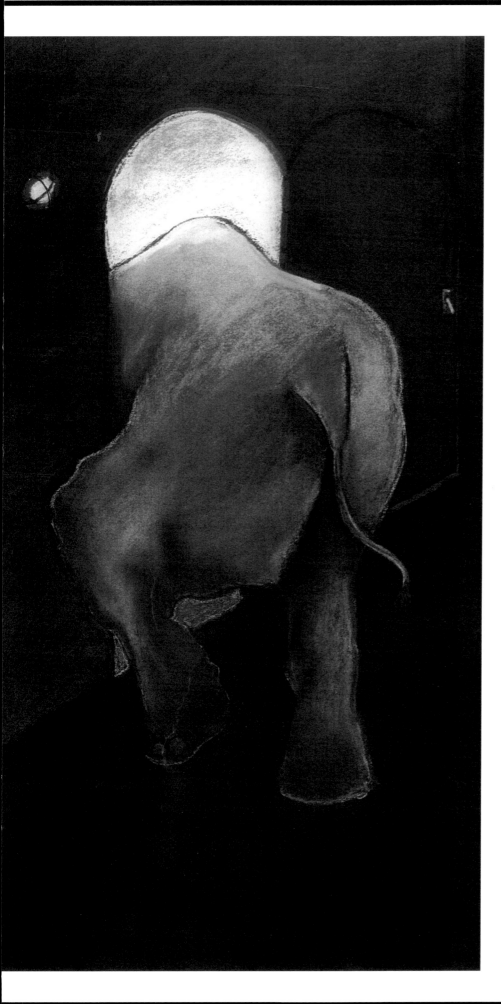

As Randy moved to the captain's chair, his arms shook; it was difficult to put on the headset. "Uncle Jim, I can't land the plane by myself," Randy's voice trembled.

"You must," Uncle Jim shouted. "Let's tune into air traffic tower."

Suddenly a voice from the headphones spoke. "San Diego tower here. Do you need some help?"

Randy explained to the tower that his uncle was stuck behind an elephant and he had to land the plane by himself. There was a pause. "How are you flying?" asked the tower.

"Auto pilot," Randy responded.

Just then Uncle Jim peered over Sally's back. He raised his voice to be heard over her loud snorting. "Randy, we will be safe. Just follow our instructions."

"First, hold on tightly to the steering wheel and switch the auto pilot to off," Uncle Jim said. The voice over the headphones spoke again."You are headed in the right direction. Look for the runway lights and as you descend, watch for runway number eight. You will use the runway to land."

Randy looked out the window. The city lights looked like bright jewels tossed onto a warm blanket. Off in the distance, he saw the brilliant runway lights. "I see it! I see it!" Randy shouted. Randy's eyes frantically looked for runway number eight. Again he yelled, "I see it! I see it." His hands trembled as he lowered the flaps and the landing gear.

As the landing gear fell in place, Uncle Jim said, "Good job."

As the airplane began to descend, Randy knew his uncle and all the animals were counting on him. Randy's arm stiffened as he held tightly onto the steering wheel. "I can do it," Randy thought. His heart quickened at the excitement. "I must do it," he whispered.

As he approached the runway, Randy knew he must face his fears. He watched the quilt of colors become houses and streets rushing under the plane faster and faster. The engines roared in his ears, and the fumes filled his nose. Out the window he could see the runway lights brushing the tips of the wings. Suddenly number eight flashed by. "I will do it!" Randy shouted.

As Randy took in a deep breath, his fears seemed to fly away. The wheels touched ground. He pulled back on the steering wheel with all his strength and eased up on the throttle. He pressed firmly down on the brakes, and he gently steered the plane to the end of the runway until it stopped. Randy looked out the window and saw cars with flashing lights racing toward the plane.

The airport police boarded the airplane and pulled Sally out into the cargo area. As they exited the airplane, everyone shook Randy's hand. He felt very proud of what he had done.

"Congratulations, you have definitely earned this pair of wings, Captain Randy," Uncle Jim said. His uncle took off his captain's wings and proudly pinned the bright pair of golden wings on Randy's shirt.

Randy and Uncle Jim got into a waiting car and watched the ground crew unload the animals. Randy waved to Manny and Sally through the window. Randy let out a weary sigh. As he sank back into the car seat, again the voices became faint whispers and he could not fight sleep.

"Randy, dear, wake up." His mother
gently touched his forehead. "Randy,
you must have had an exciting dream.
You were giggling and wiggling in your
sleep," she said.

"Mom, I flew an airplane!" he exclaimed.

"Oh, Randy," his mother teased.

"No, Mom. Really, I flew an airplane with
Uncle Jim. There were these animals . . ."

"Randy, what an imagination you have,"
she said as she turned to walk away.
She didn't notice the brilliant gleam of light
near the pocket of Randy's pajamas.

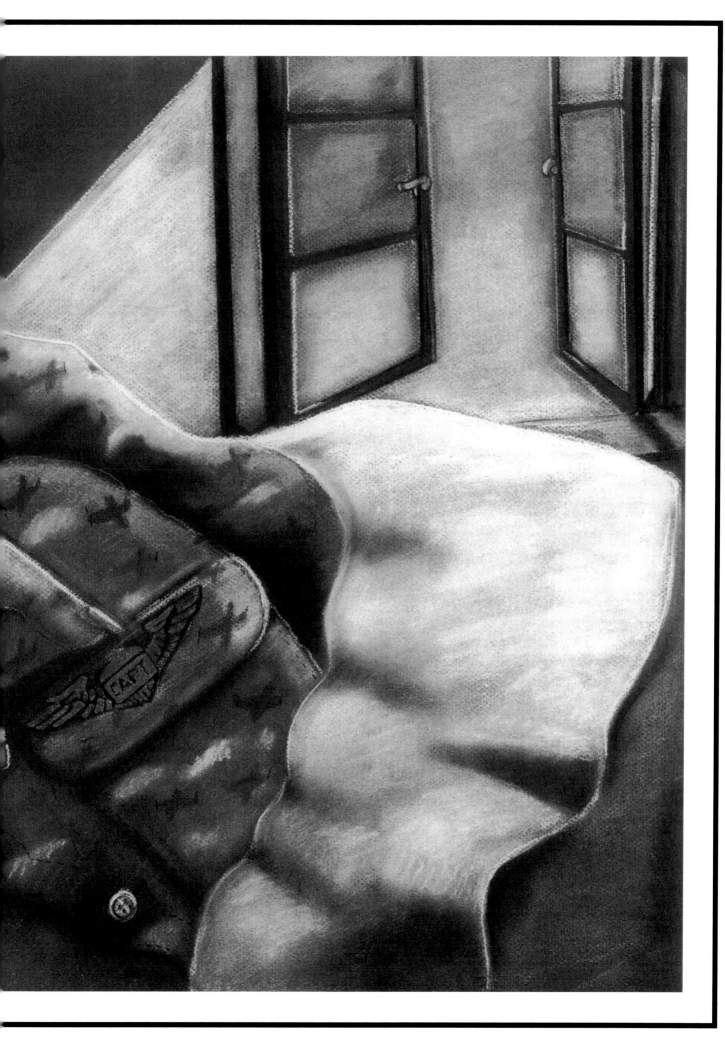